For my family,
Kelly, Benjamin, and Edward.

And for my high school art teacher,
Mrs. Elam.

• A NOTE ON THE ART •

Each piece of art begins with a rough pencil sketch projected onto a piece of glass as a guide for sculpting. The illustration is shaped in clay by hand, then wooden tools are used to create the smallest details. The clay sculptures are photographed outdoors in natural light and then digitally painted with as little retouching as possible. I can say my fingerprints are literally all over this book!

Although the worlds in this book live in my head, when I sculpt them in clay they become real. I can touch them, light them, and look at them from different angles. Each clay sculpture takes its own time to create. Whether I am sculpting the trees or clouds or characters, I feel like I am truly immersed in this little world. It's real to me. I just love it.

BLOOMSBURY CHILDREN'S BOOKS
Bloomsbury Publishing Inc., part of Bloomsbury Publishing Plc
1385 Broadway, New York, NY 10018

BLOOMSBURY, BLOOMSBURY CHILDREN'S BOOKS, and the Diana logo are trademarks of Bloomsbury Publishing Plc

First published in the United States of America in February 2021
by Bloomsbury Children's Books

Text and illustrations copyright © 2021 by Andy Harkness

Bloomsbury books may be purchased for business or promotional use. For information on bulk purchases please contact Macmillan Corporate and Premium Sales Department at specialmarkets@macmillan.com

Library of Congress Cataloging-in-Publication Data
available upon request
ISBN 978-1-5476-0442-5 (hardcover) • ISBN 978-1-5476-0443-2 (e-book) • ISBN 978-1-5476-0444-9 (e-PDF)

Typeset in Niramit SemiBold and Londrina
Book design by John Candell
Printed in China by Leo Paper Products, Heshan, Guangdong
2 4 6 8 10 9 7 5 3 1

All papers used by Bloomsbury Publishing Plc are natural, recyclable products made from wood grown in well-managed forests. The manufacturing processes conform to the environmental regulations of the country of origin.

To find out more about our authors and books visit www.bloomsbury.com and sign up for our newsletters.

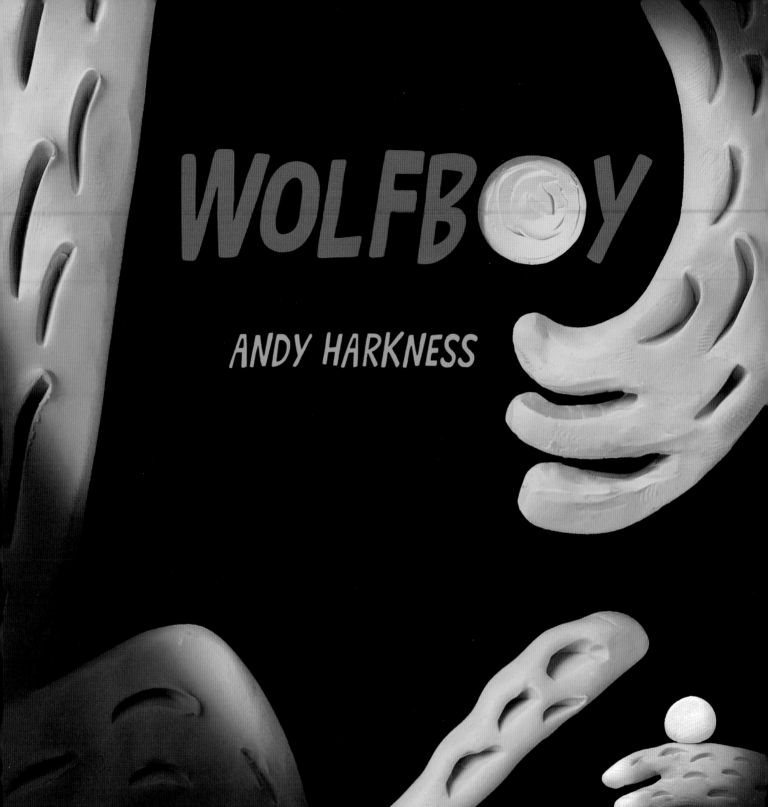

WOLFBOY

ANDY HARKNESS

BLOOMSBURY
CHILDREN'S BOOKS
NEW YORK LONDON OXFORD NEW DELHI SYDNEY

The moon was full.

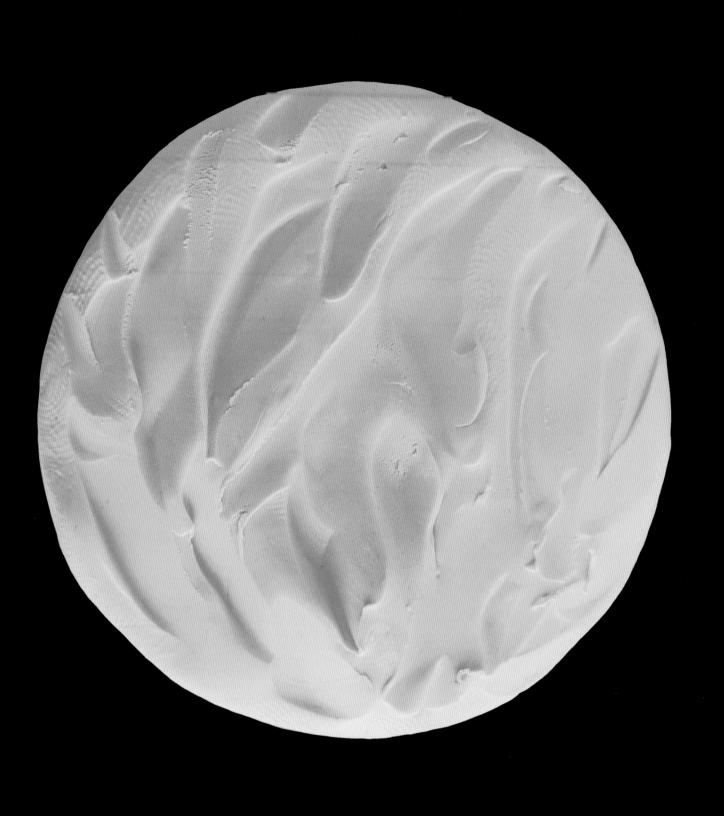

Wolfboy stomped beneath the shadowy trees.
He was **HUNGRY**.

"Rabbits, rabbits! Where are you?" he howled.
But the rabbits were nowhere to be found.

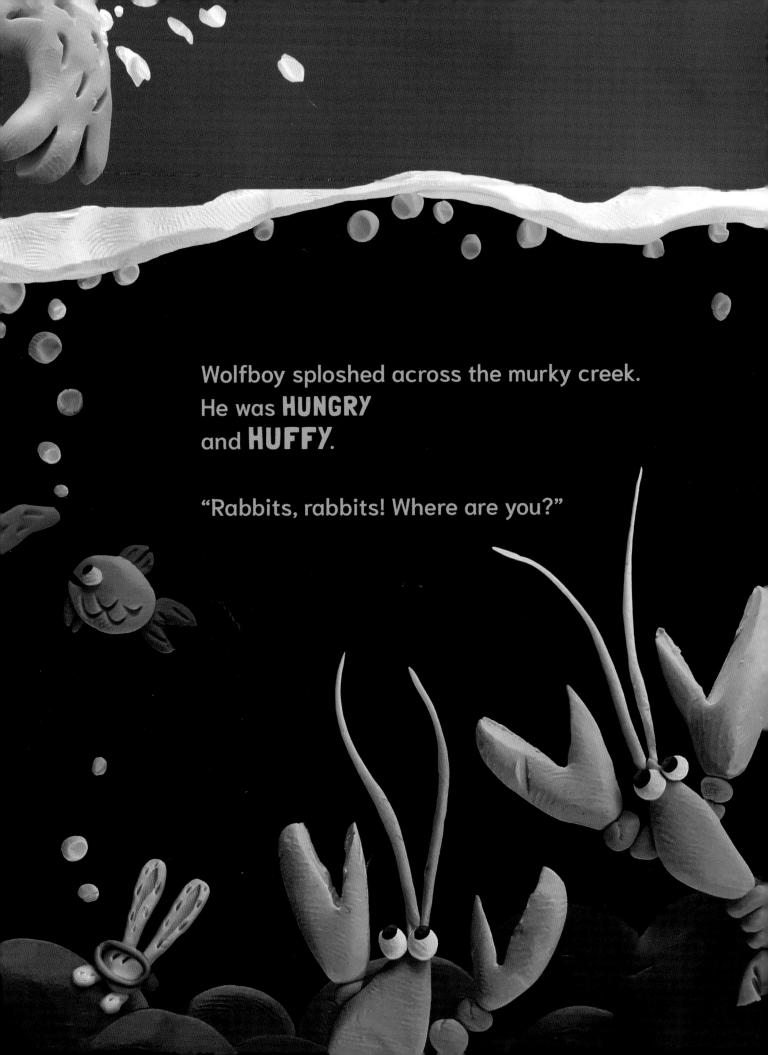

Wolfboy sploshed across the murky creek.
He was **HUNGRY**
and **HUFFY**.

"Rabbits, rabbits! Where are you?"

Wolfboy climbed up the creaky old oak.

He was **HUNGRY**
and **HUFFY**
and **DROOLY**.

He needed rabbits.

"Rabbits, rabbits! Where are you?"

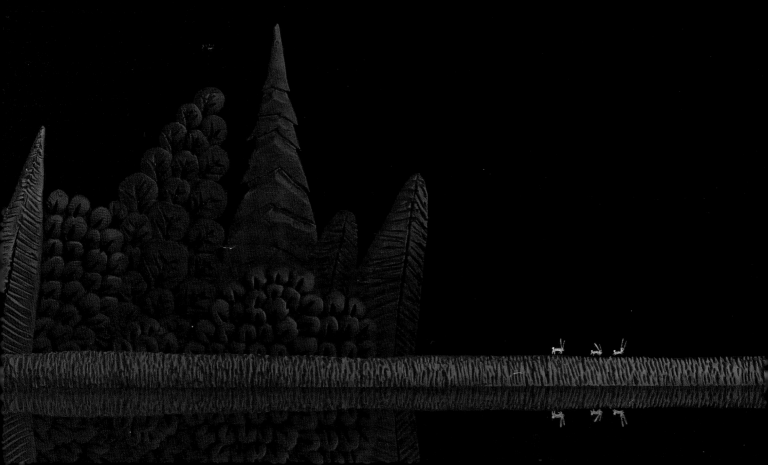

Wolfboy slogged through the soggy bog.

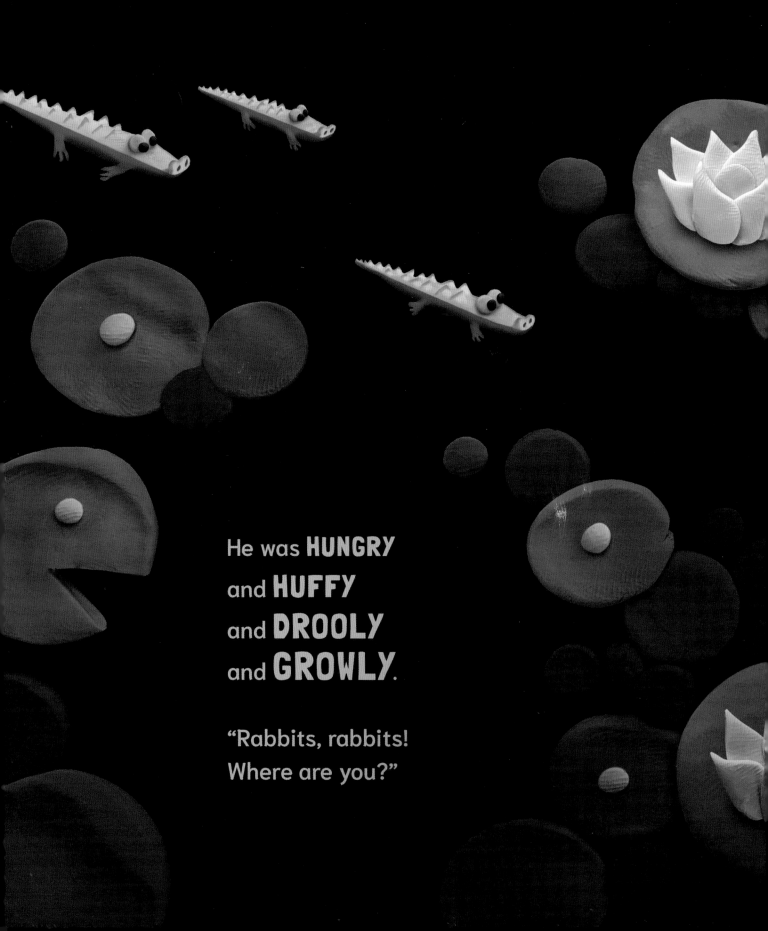

He was **HUNGRY**
and **HUFFY**
and **DROOLY**
and **GROWLY**.

"Rabbits, rabbits!
Where are you?"

Wolfboy leaped across

the steep ravine . . .

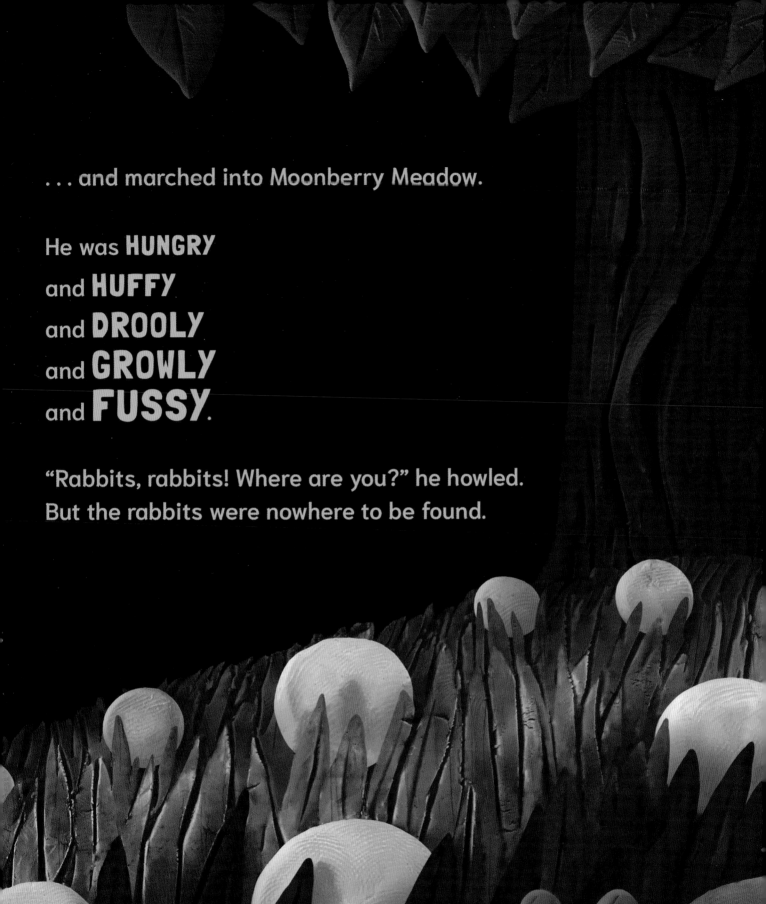

. . . and marched into Moonberry Meadow.

He was **HUNGRY**
and **HUFFY**
and **DROOLY**
and **GROWLY**
and **FUSSY**.

"Rabbits, rabbits! Where are you?" he howled.
But the rabbits were nowhere to be found.

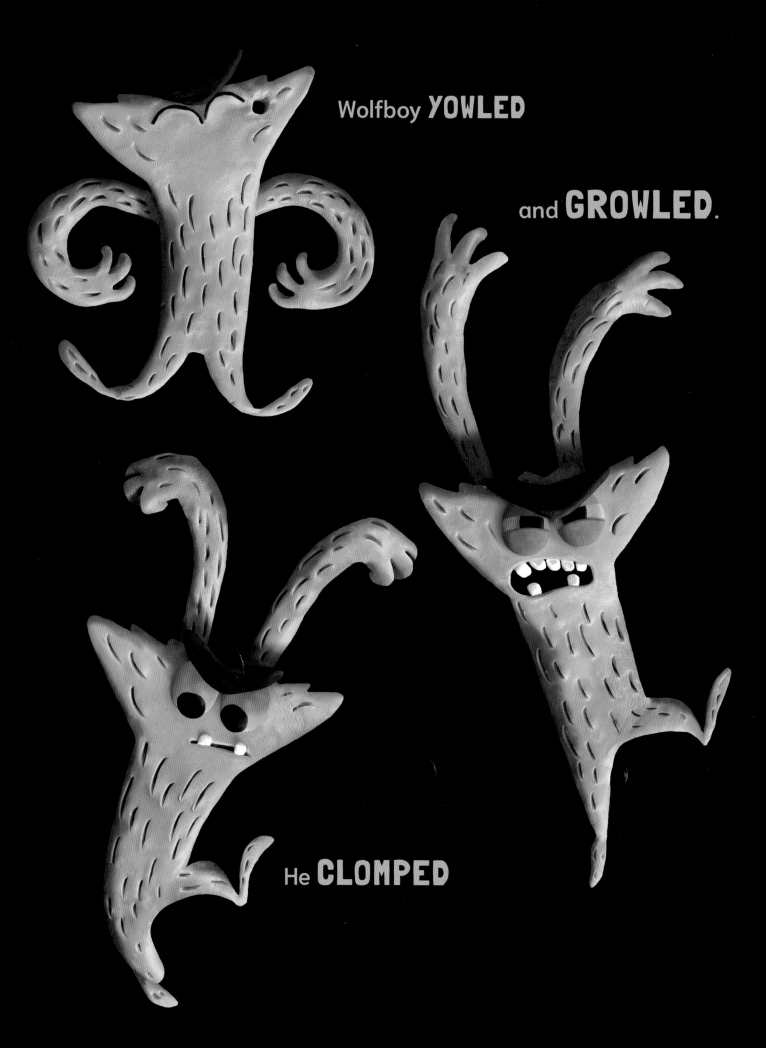

Wolfboy **YOWLED**

and **GROWLED**.

He **CLOMPED**

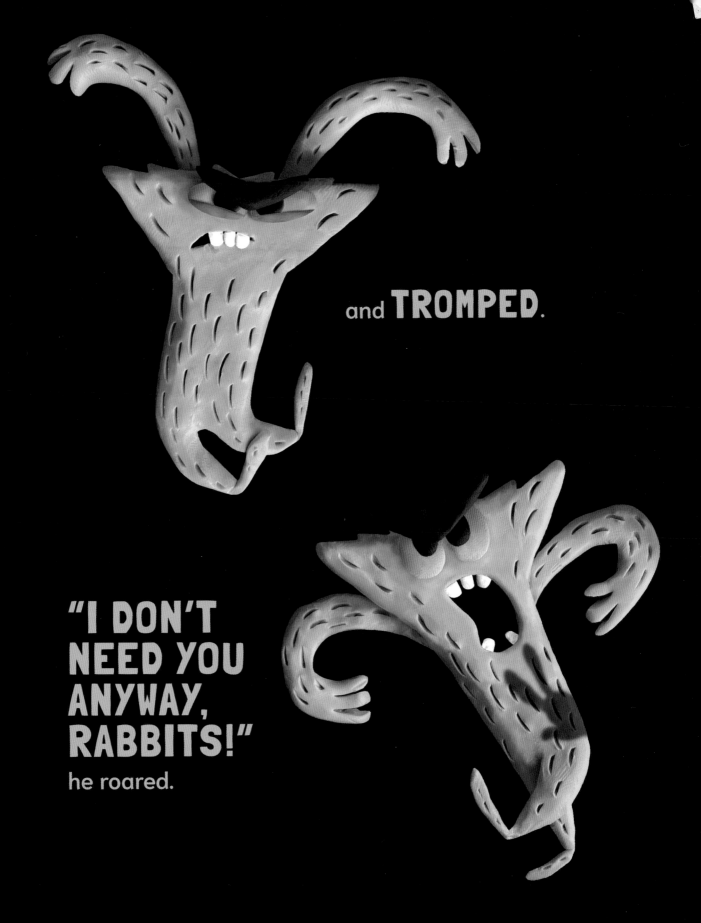

and **TROMPED**.

"I DON'T NEED YOU ANYWAY, RABBITS!"

he roared.

Suddenly, there was a rustle of grass.

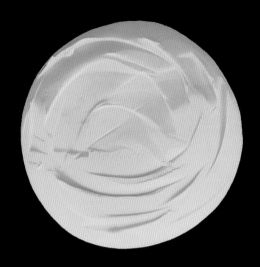

Wolfboy froze.

A twig snapped.

Wolfboy's eyes sharpened.

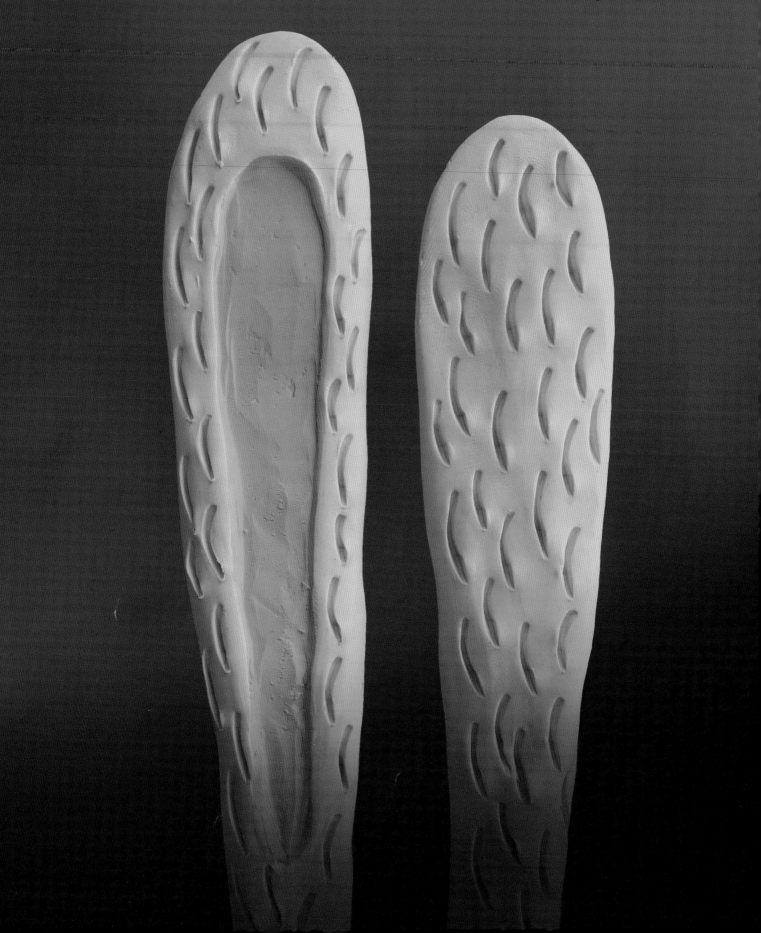

Then he saw two long ears . . .

A furry foot.

And a cottony tail.

Wolfboy
crouched
low.

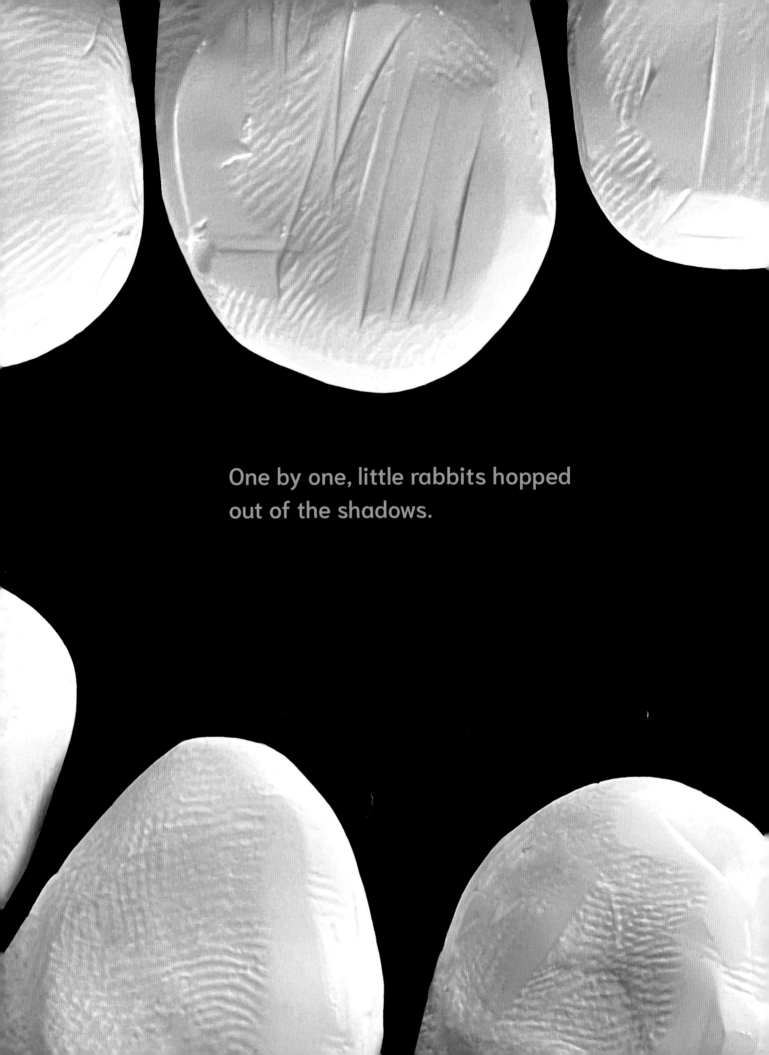

One by one, little rabbits hopped out of the shadows.

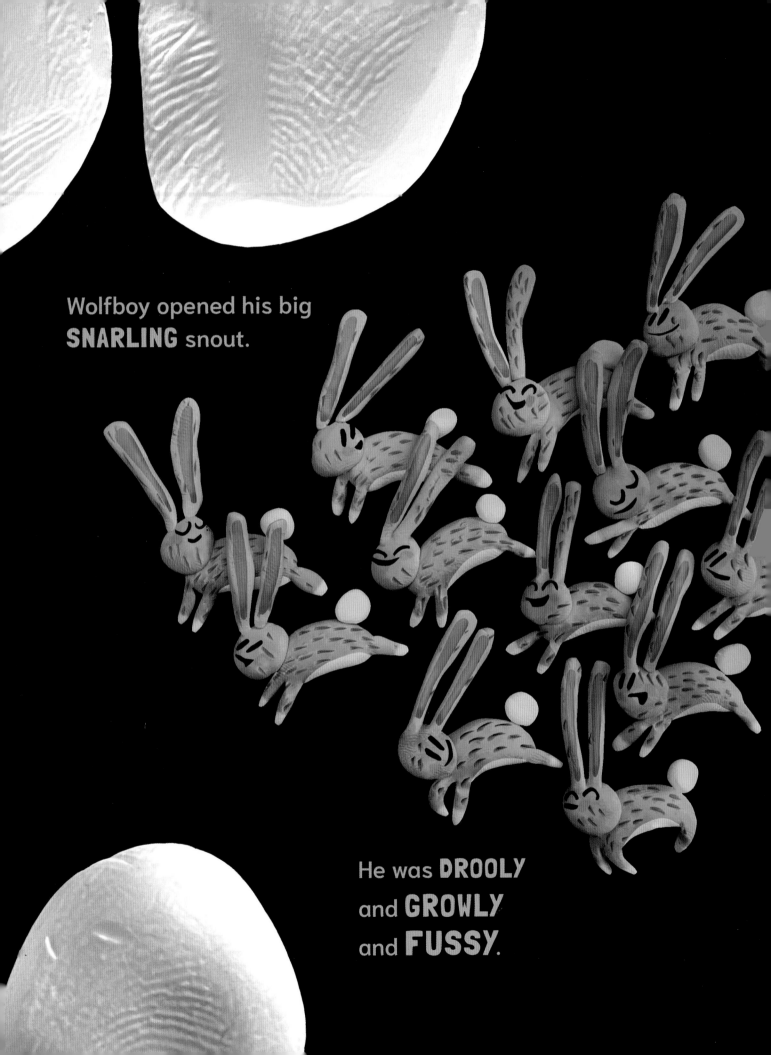

Wolfboy opened his big
SNARLING snout.

He was **DROOLY**
and **GROWLY**
and **FUSSY**.

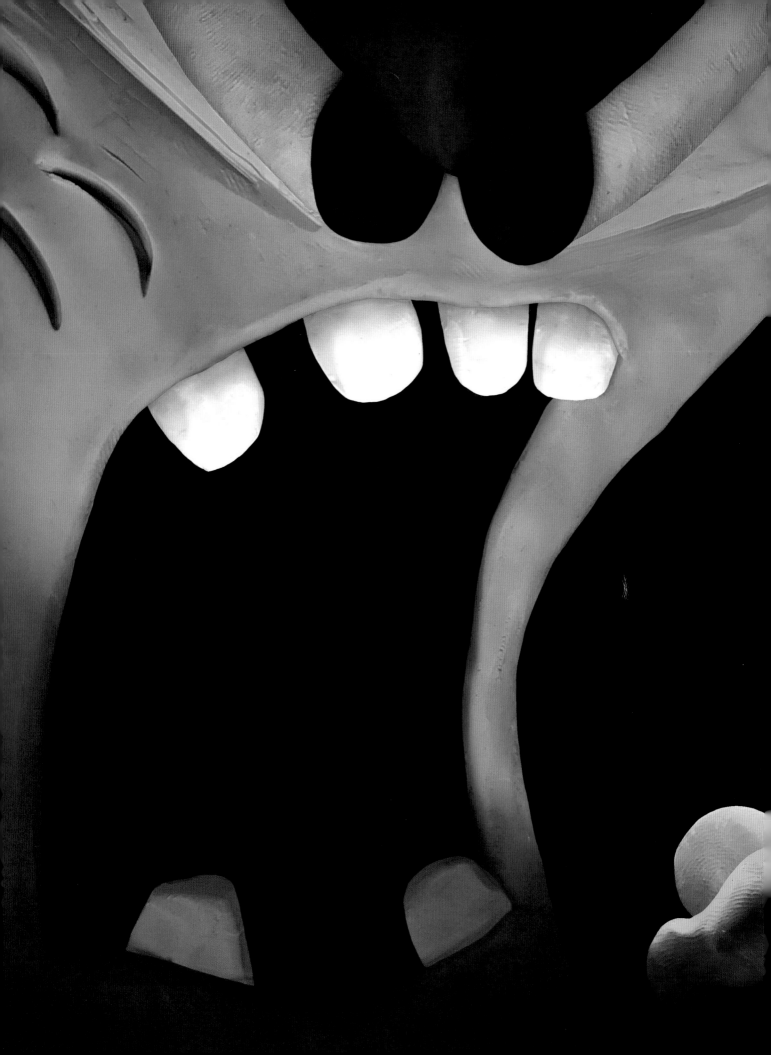

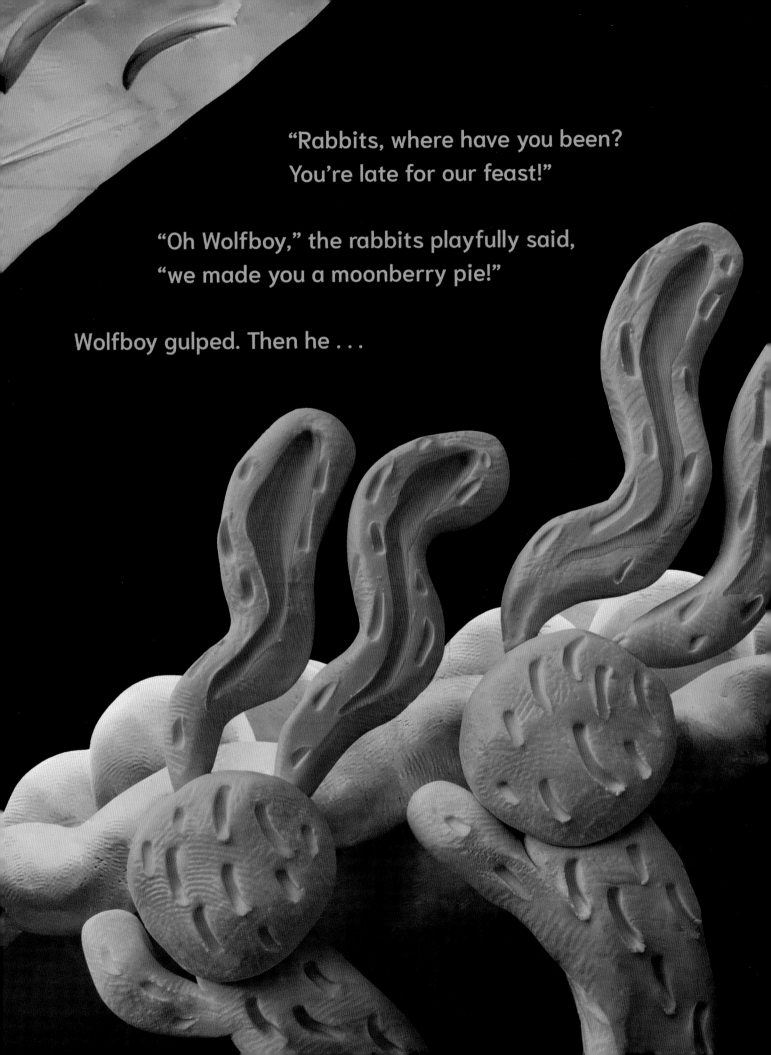

"Rabbits, where have you been?
You're late for our feast!"

"Oh Wolfboy," the rabbits playfully said,
"we made you a moonberry pie!"

Wolfboy gulped. Then he . . .

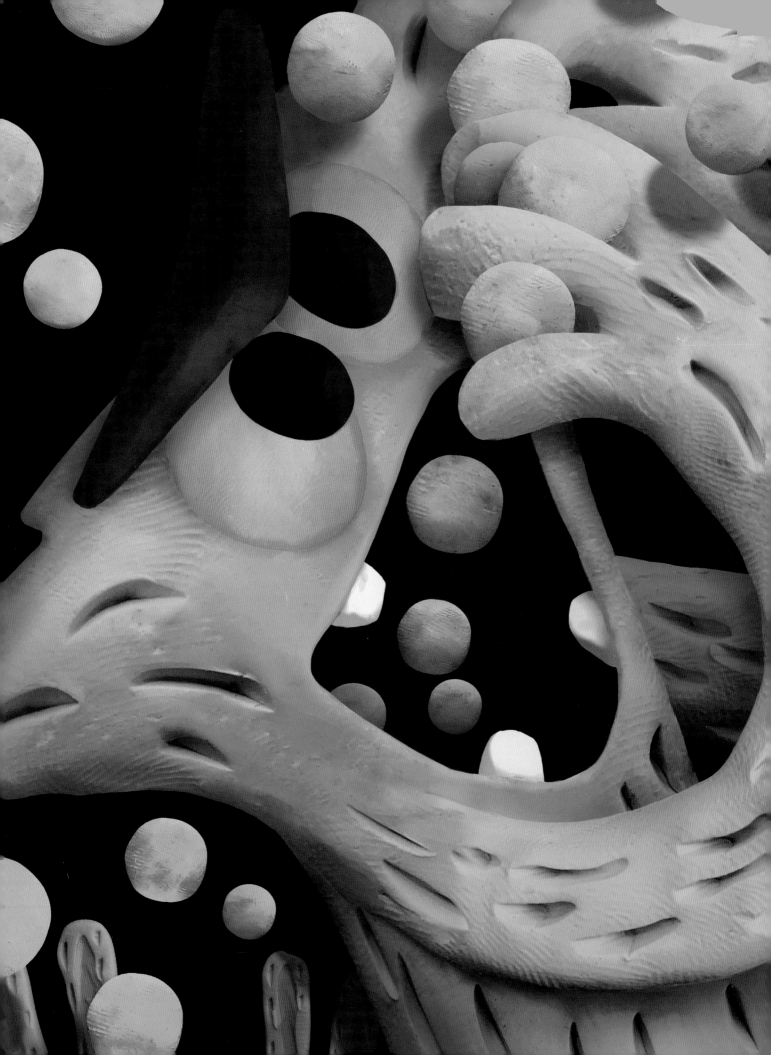

...CRUNCHED
and MUNCHED
and GOBBLED
and GULPED!

"Rabbits, I was just so **HUNGRY**
and **HUFFY**
and **DROOLY**
and **GROWLY**
and **FUSSY**."

"And don't forget **HOWLY!**"
the rabbits said.

"But now I am . . .